Contents

Chapter One
The Missing Medal

"Guess what!" Titus McKay said
to his cousins Timothy and Sarah-Jane
as soon as they got in the door.

"My baby-sitter Jake
got a ferret named Freddie!
Jake said I could bring you over
to play with him."

Titus was crazy about animals.
And animals were crazy about him.

Sarah-Jane and Timothy
looked a little doubtful.

They didn't want to admit it.
But they weren't too sure what a ferret was.

"He's very friendly," said Titus.

"Oh," said Sarah-Jane.

"Well, as long as he's friendly…"

Titus lived in an apartment building.
So all the cousins had to do
was walk down the hall
and knock on Jake's door.

Freddie was sacked out in his hammock
when they got there.

"Isn't he cute?" said Titus.
"Ferrets sleep a lot.
But he'll soon get up for playtime."

There were other interesting things
in Jake's apartment.

"Hey, Jake," said Titus.
"Can I show Tim and S-J
your swimming medal?"

"Sure," said Jake.
"It's right there on the hall table.
My mom set it out to get it framed."

"I don't see it," said Titus.
Neither did Timothy and Sarah-Jane.
And the cousins were very good
at noticing things.

Jake came over to take a look.

"That's odd," he said.
"It was right there yesterday
when my friend Bill came over."

Jake thought about it a minute.

"I remember that I had Freddie out
for playtime, and—"

Titus and Jake looked at each other.

They said the exact same thing
at the exact same time.

"FREDDIE!"

Chapter Two
Hiding Places

"*Freddie?*" said Sarah-Jane and Timothy at the exact same time.

They wondered what a ferret had to do with a missing swimming medal.

"Oh…uh, right," said Titus. "I guess I forgot to tell you something. There's this little thing that Freddie does. All ferrets do it. It's kind of cute, actually. I mean, it wouldn't be cute if a *person* did it. But Freddie doesn't know any better."

"Ti!" said Sarah-Jane.

"What in the *world* are you talking about?"

Titus sighed.

"Freddie is such a sweet little guy.
But he...um...steals stuff."

"*What?*" cried Sarah-Jane.

"*Why?*" asked Timothy.

Jake shrugged.

"Who knows?" he said.
"Freddie just loves to take things.
Then he puts them
in his favorite hiding places."

"He loves dirty socks," said Titus.
"Dirty socks always go under the chair."

Jake added, "And all the other stuff
goes behind the sofa."

Without another word,
Jake and the cousins
got to work.

The cousins were very good
at finding things.

And they were even better than Jake
at squeezing into small places.

Sure enough, Jake found two dirty socks under the chair.

And the cousins found quite a lot of stuff behind the sofa.

A pen.

A bracelet.

A set of keys.

A shoe.

"Wow! Just look at all the stuff he took!" said Timothy.

"How did he do it?" asked Sarah-Jane.

"He's very sneaky," said Jake
as he got Freddie out of his cage.
"I'll have to watch him more closely."

Titus looked at the cute little ferret.
He looked at the pile of stuff on the floor.
Then he said what they were all thinking.

"Freddie, what did you do with the
medal?"

Chapter Three
Out in the Hall

Jake said, "You're so sneaky, Freddie. You must have found a new hiding place just for the medal. Now I have to look all over for it. I just hope you didn't chew up the ribbon."

Titus could tell that Jake was pretty worried.

So he said, "Jake, do you want to look for the medal some more? We could take Freddie out to play in the hall."

Freddie's favorite game
in the whole world was "Chase."
    First Titus held on to Freddie's leash.
Then he and Freddie chased
Timothy and Sarah-Jane down the hall.

Then Timothy took the leash.
And he and Freddie chased
Sarah-Jane and Titus up the hall.
Then Sarah-Jane took the leash.
And she and Freddie chased
Titus and Timothy down the hall.

The game wasn't that hard.
Except you had to run quietly
so the neighbors wouldn't get mad.
And not yelling
while you were being chased
by a ferret
was pretty hard.
When they stopped to rest,
Sarah-Jane said,
"You know, Freddie really *is* cute.
It looks like he's wearing a little mask."
"Which makes sense," said Timothy.
"Because he's a little robber.
Are you a little robber, Freddie?"
Freddie looked up.
Just as innocent as could be.

Then it was Titus's turn
to take the leash again.
They turned around to head back.
And they saw someone
go into Jake's apartment.

Chapter Four
Something Odd

"Who's that?" Timothy asked.

"Jake's friend Bill," said Titus.

"I wonder what he's doing here."

"Just visiting?" said Sarah-Jane.

"I guess so," said Titus.

"Let's go see."

Titus picked up Freddie

and carried him back to the apartment.

"You know Bill, right?" Jake asked them.

Bill was sitting on the sofa.

He nodded at them.

And the cousins said, "Hi."

"Any luck?" Titus asked Jake.

"Nope," said Jake.

"I stopped looking just now
when Bill came by.
And I got out some of Freddie's toys.
Maybe if we keep him busy,
he won't be able to steal anything else."

So the cousins got down on the floor
to play with Freddie.

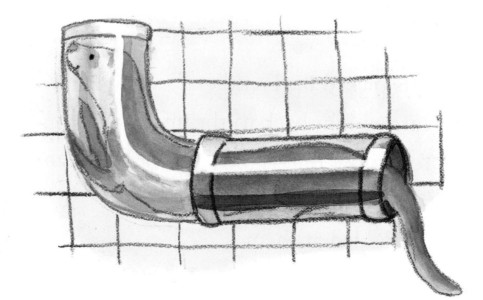

When they were down there,
Titus saw something odd.
Something very odd indeed.
He rushed to the sofa
and grabbed something up in his hand.
"What is it?" everyone asked.

Titus opened his hand
and showed them the medal.

"Where did *that* come from?" cried Jake.

"I don't know," said Titus. "All I know
is that the medal wasn't under the sofa
when we looked before."

"Then how did it get there?"
asked Sarah-Jane. "Did Freddie move it?"

"He couldn't have," said Titus.
"He was either in his cage
or out in the hall the whole time.
He has an *alibi*. Us."

"Well," said Bill. "I've got to get
going."

"Not so fast," said Titus.

Chapter Five
Lost and Found

Titus said to Bill,

"You were here yesterday when Jake
left the medal on the hall table.
And you were here today
when I found the medal under the sofa.
I think you took the medal yesterday.
And you brought it back today.
But you didn't put it back on the table.
You knew Jake might figure out you took it.
So you put it in Freddie's hiding place.
You wanted Jake to think that
Freddie took it!"

Titus took a deep breath.

"Except Freddie wouldn't have put
the medal *under* the sofa.
He puts stuff like that *behind* the sofa.
And he would have chewed up the ribbon.
This ribbon is not chewed up at all.
Freddie didn't take the medal.
You did."

Bill's face turned a little pink.

"Maybe I sort of *borrowed* it," he said.

"Why?" asked Jake.

Bill's face turned *very* pink.

"Well, see, these people were coming over, and I sort of set it out at my place."

"Why?" asked Timothy.

"So they would think it was *your* medal?"

Bill's face turned even pinker.

He said to Jake,

"Hey, look, man, I'm really sorry."

"It's OK," said Jake. "Forget about it."

But Titus was still mad.

"YOU FRAMED AN INNOCENT FERRET!"

There was a moment of silence.

Then Timothy and Sarah-Jane
burst out laughing.

So did Jake and Bill.

And finally, so did Titus.

As for Freddie—
he was already dozing off.
He'd had enough excitement
for one day.

The End